APR 1 2018

D0393751

THE CREEPER DIARIES

SPECIAL EDITION

CREEPIN' THROUGH THE SNOW

Also by Greyson Mann:

The Creeper Diaries

Mob School Survivor

Creeper's Got Talent

Secrets of an Overworld Survivor

Lost in the Jungle

When Lava Strikes

Wolves vs. Zombies

Never Say Nether

The Witch's Warning

THE CREEPER DIARIES

SPECIAL EDITION

CREEPIN' THROUGH THE SNOW

GREYSON MANN
ILLUSTRATED BY AMANDA BRACK

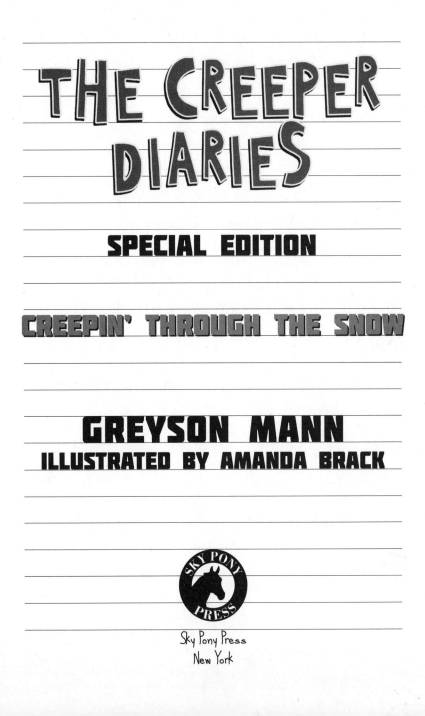

Sky Pony Press
New York

Sky Pony Press books may be purchased in bulk at special discounts for sales promotion, corporate gifts, fund-raising, or educational purposes. Special editions can also be created to specifications. For details, contact the Special Sales Department, Sky Pony Press, 307 West 36th Street, 11th Floor, New York, NY 10018 or info@skyhorsepublishing.com.

Sky Pony® is a registered trademark of Skyhorse Publishing, Inc.®, a Delaware corporation.

Visit our website at www.skyponypress.com.

10 9 8 7 6 5 4 3 2 1

Library of Congress Cataloging-in-Publication Data is available on file.

Special thanks to Erin L. Falligant.

Cover illustration by Amanda Brack
Cover design by Brian Peterson

Hardcover ISBN: 978-1-5107-2734-2
E-book ISBN: 978-1-5107-2735-9

Printed in the United States of America

DAY 1: FRIDAY

Mom says the holidays are when miracles happen. She sure wasn't kidding. I saw one with my own eyes tonight.

We had just finished stuffing ourselves with mushroom stew—AGAIN. That's what we eat for Thanksgiving, to celebrate the time when mobs and miners came together in peace. Dad leaned back in his chair, and I could tell he was about to launch into his story about the olden days, when only MOBS roamed the Overworld. Before miners came and battles broke out.

Well, I've heard that story a gazillion times just this past week alone. I guess Mom was tired of it too, because she stood up and said we should do something fun as a family—SHOPPING!

That's how I ended up on the street by the Creeper Café, where the miracle happened.

See, Mom gave me and my sisters a bunch of emeralds to buy gifts for Creeper's Eve.

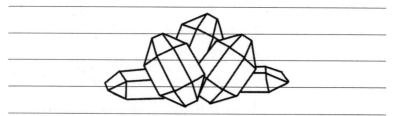

That's December 31, when we all creep around and hide presents for each other to celebrate the new year. I don't exactly love buying gifts for my sisters. But if I shop smart, I'll have enough emeralds left to buy something for MYSELF.

My teenage sister must have had the same idea, because she disappeared into the Skins R Us store by the café. Cate is always trying out different wigs and skins. She's got a whole closet full of them at home.

Chloe, my Evil Twin, disappeared too. I really wish she'd do that more often. (We haven't gotten along since, like, Halloween.)

Then Mom and Dad hurried into the candy store with Cammy before she blew up with excitement. I knew my baby sister would want blaze powder candies.

They're so hot, they'd make her blow up anyway. But I didn't point that out.

Like I said, when your parents offer you emeralds, you don't argue. You just grin and walk away before they make you put the emeralds in your piggy bank or something.

An emerald saved is an emerald earned!

So I headed down the street toward the fireworks store. I figured if my family saw me coming out of there, it would give them a huge hint about what I want for Creeper's Eve. Fireworks to ring in the new year, please!

But as I passed the toy store, guess who popped out?
My good friend Sam the Slime. And he was dragging
something behind him: a new Nether brick-red sled.

"That's dumb," I said before I could stop myself. "It
NEVER snows down here in the plains."

Any other mob might have gotten mad. But my words
bounced right off that jolly slime. He said he wasn't
waiting for snow. He was going to make an ice slide.

Well, THAT sounded pretty cool. I wanted a piece
of that action. In fact, now I wanted a sled too. A
bigger one. A faster one. A greener one. And there
it was, right there in the store window!

Staring at that sled, I could already picture me
zooming around the snowy mountains of the Taiga.

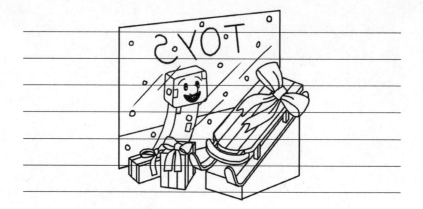

And that's when the miracle happened.

A snowflake drifted out of the sky and *plopped* onto my forehead. I'm not even kidding. It dribbled right down my cheek like a tear of joy.

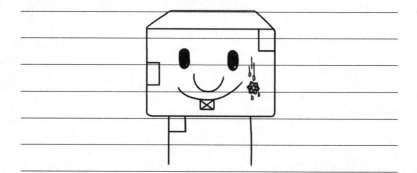

And that snow kept right on coming. It snowed so hard, we didn't even have to go to school tonight. We had our first official Snow Night!

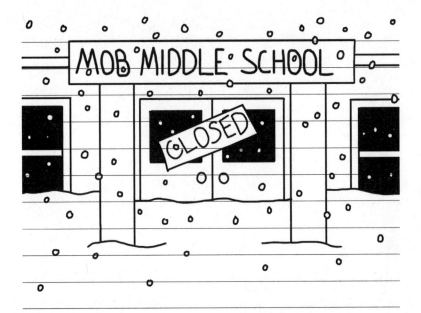

Of course, we all went to school anyway to play in the snow. There's this big hill behind Mob Middle School, and I couldn't wait to ride on Sam's sled. But when I got there, he said there wasn't enough room on it for me. Say WHAT?

I tried to prove him wrong. I stretched myself out until I was long and skinny. I rolled into a ball and tried to sit on his lap. But no matter how I twisted and turned, I couldn't fit on that sled with Sam.

So I did what any friend would do. I asked *him* to get off. I mean, what does a slime need with a sled anyway? He'd probably have more fun BOUNCING down the hill.

Before I could say so, the sled DISAPPEARED. Someone swiped it right out from under us! And then Bones was zooming down the hill, laughing his bony skeleton butt off.

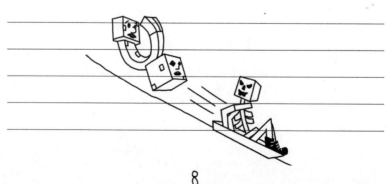

Sam waited for a while, as if Bones and his gang of spider jockeys were actually going to bring that sled back. But I knew better. So I decided to do something I've always wanted to do—build a snow golem. And when Sam saw me rolling a snowball, he forgot all about his sled and bounced over to help.

Ziggy Zombie helped too. He's about the grossest kid I know, but I owe him big because he's the one who found a couple of Jack o' Lanterns to use for the snow golems' heads.

Those pumpkins must have been left over from Halloween. They were black and rotten around the eyes, and the back sides were half eaten, like critters had made dinner out of them. I don't even WANT to know what was crawling around INSIDE.

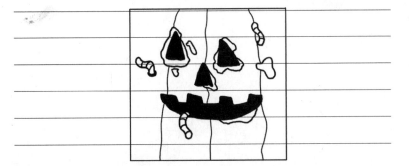

But when Ziggy put the Jack o' Lanterns on the snow golems' bodies, it worked! Those golems actually came to life. They stared right at me and started sliding around in the snow.

I was pretty sure I'd died and gone to creeper heaven, until—

SMACK!

An icy snowball hit me square between the eyes.

"Gotcha, Itchy!"

Yup, that was Bones again, sailing by on Sam's sled. The nickname stung—my name is NOT Itchy, it's Gerald. And that snowball hit me HARD. Who knew you could shoot snowballs with a bow?

Pretty soon, all his spider jockey friends joined the fight, and Sam and I were in a battle for our lives. So I did what any smart creeper would do. I hid.

Sam tried to hide between the snow golems too, but there wasn't even CLOSE to enough room. So I pushed him back out. When in danger, it's every mob for himself.

Those snowballs kept coming, bouncing off Sam left and right. He was one big jiggling slime ball. He didn't know which way to turn!

Then another miracle happened. Our friends the snow golems started throwing snowballs BACK at Bones.

He was a pretty good shot too. The good news is, the golems chased those skeletons right down the hill, and they never came back. The bad news is, they took Sam's sled with them.

Sam wasn't all that happy with me after that. The slime kind of gave me the cold shoulder, actually. Until his girlfriend, Willow Witch, showed up.

Personally, I think Sam's kind of young to be dating an eighth-grade witch. But every once in a while, it's kind of nice to have her around. Like tonight, when Sam was acting all mopey. She cheered him up by saying, "Do you want to make snow spiders? I'll show you."

Willow plopped onto her back and swept her arms and legs up and down. When she stood up, she'd left a mark in the snow that KIND of looked like a spider. So we all tried it—even Ziggy Zombie.

I wasn't totally happy with my snow spider. But then I looked at Sam's and felt a whole lot better about mine.

And while I was lying there beside him, staring up at the snowflakes, I had an epiphany. Dad says that's when an idea strikes, like lightning from the sky.

I decided that the snowstorm was a SIGN—a sign that I HAD to buy that sled in the toy store. NOW.

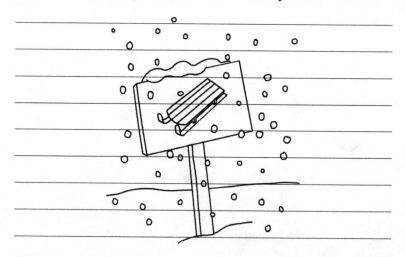

So I raced back to the store and bought that shiny green sled. I sneaked it home without anyone noticing. Well, my pet squid Sticky noticed. He stared at the sled from his aquarium. Then he turned his beady little eyes toward me. Was he trying to make me feel guilty?

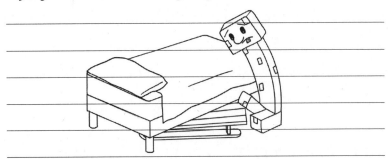

Sure, I'd spent every emerald Mom had given me for Creeper's Eve gifts. "But it's worth it," I told Sticky. "Don't judge."

And it WAS worth it, until I realized someone else had seen me bring that sled home. My Evil Twin.

Suddenly, Chloe was all up in my face, threatening to tell Mom and Dad. So I did what I had to do. I broke open my piggy bank and bribed her with my last couple of emeralds just to keep her quiet.

But now that she's gone and the sled is hidden under my bed, I'm freaking out. I mean, Creeper's Eve is only 30 days away. And I have a couple of important things to do before then.

So it's time for a plan. Here's what I'm thinking:

30-Day Plan for the Holidays

- Find a way to get more emeralds

- Buy Creeper's Eve gifts (but NOT for Chloe!!!)

- Keep my Evil Twin quiet about the sled thing

That's a pretty good plan. But a creeper's gotta have SOME fun, right? So maybe I'll add one more thing to the list:

· Become the greatest sledding creeper of ALL time

Hey, it's the holidays. And I'm here to tell you, miracles can happen!

DAY 3: SUNDAY (MORNING)

I sure had a good day's sleep after all that fun
in the snow. But I woke up last night to a total
NIGHTMARE—a hissing green face with gaping eyes
and a twisted smile. It took me a few seconds to
realize it was just my sister Chloe.

She was sitting on my new sled, and she had a
demand. "Give me an emerald."

I reminded her that I already HAD given her one
yesterday.

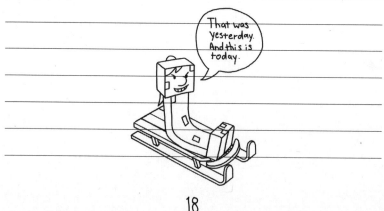

I think she's been watching WAY too many action flicks with Dad lately.

So I marched over to my broken piggybank and showed her that I was fresh out of emeralds, thanks to her.

She said that wasn't her problem and that I needed to pay her an emerald a day, EVERY day, or she was gonna tell Mom and Dad what I did with all the emeralds they gave me.

SERIOUSLY??? I've said it before and I'll say it again. There's NO WAY that creep is my twin. I couldn't have shared an egg with her for even a second. I would have blasted my way out, for sure.

At least now that we're older, I can tell her to get out of my room. So I did. And I slid the sled back under my bed.

Then I sat there trying to figure out how I was going to make enough emeralds to buy presents for Creeper's Eve AND pay off Chloe to keep her big mouth shut.

I came up with all kinds of genius ideas for how to earn emeralds.

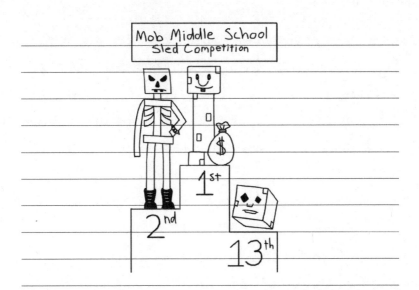

But every single one had something to do with my new sled. The one hiding under my bed. The one that I probably won't be able to use. EVER.

So after dinner, I asked my dad for advice on how to get a job.

Chloe was on dish duty, and I hoped she wouldn't hear me over the running water. But she must have, because she snorted and gave me a smirk. She probably felt super powerful, like it was all because of her that I was looking for ways to kick-start my career.

But I just ignored her and looked the other way. Which brought me face to face with Cate. YIKES.

I guess when we went shopping the other night, she bought herself a brand-new look. I gotta say, I'm not really loving the spiky green wig. But I learned a long time ago that if I can't say something nice about Cate's new looks, I should just keep my creeper mouth shut.

Dad seemed all proud that I was looking for work. He said maybe I could help him clear snow on the creeper cul-de-sac where we live.

I wasn't so sure about that. I mean, if it's SNOWING outside, I've really got to hit the sledding hills. That's the only way I'm ever going to become the Overworld's greatest sledding creeper. But I told Dad I appreciated his suggestion.

When Mom heard me talking about getting a job, she got all teary-eyed and said we were growing up way too fast.

And she added that we really needed to spend more family time together this year, because pretty soon my sisters and I would be all grown-up and would move away to the Extreme Hills or something.

Well, I knew I had to get out of there—FAST—before she decided we needed to spend a family night together. I had places to go and things to do and emeralds to earn. So I said that I was meeting Sam over at the sledding hill again tonight.

But Mom wasn't done with me yet. No, sirree. She told me it was cold outside and that I had to wear my super-itchy wool sweater. ARGH.

That sweater is about the ugliest thing I own. Plus, it REALLY messes with my psoriasis (SORE-EYE-A-SIS). That's just a fancy word for itchy skin. Which I have. Which is how I got the nickname "Itchy." But that's another story.

By the time I got to the sledding hill, my back was on FIRE with itchiness. I stopped at every tree I could find to give it a good scratch.

But when I saw mobs sledding down the hill and building snow forts, I remembered two things: Sam's sled, and the snow golems we'd built. Where were they?

I didn't see the golems anywhere. They must have slipped and slid off into the sunrise.

But Sam's sled was back. And so was Sam. I could hear him bawling from about fifty feet away. Yup, that slime was crying big slimy tears. His whole body was shaking and hiccupping.

Then I saw why. His sled was in BAD shape. Bones had brought it back, but he must have used it for target practice first. There were dents and scratches all over it from arrow tips—or bony skeleton fingers. A big crack ran straight across the middle.

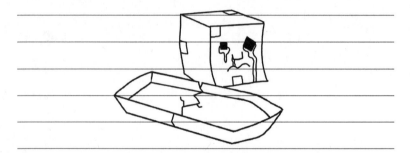

Sam looked up at me through a mess of snot and tears. I was afraid those tears would freeze on his face and end up looking like witch warts. I had to do something, FAST.

And that was when I had my most genius idea ever. I told Sam he could borrow MY sled.

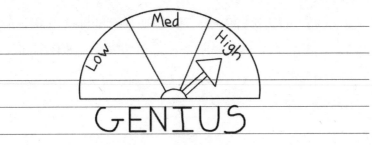

GENIUS

I know, that was pretty generous of me. But it also meant I could use my sled whenever I want. And no one would know it belongs to me. I mean, except for Chloe. But once that sled is in Sam's hands, it's Chloe's hiss against mine. My Evil Twin is going DOWN.

Sam, on the other hand, perked right up. (That slime always bounces back.) He led the way to my house to get the sled.

Luckily, Chloe was gone by then. She was probably off blowing up someone's snow fort or something.

Dad was clearing snow from the sidewalk, and Mom was helping Cammy build her own tiny snow golem in the front yard.

When Mom asked me and Sam if we knew where to find a pumpkin, we both shook our heads. The last thing I wanted was to go looking for another wormy old Jack o' Lantern. GROSS.

So I gave Cammy a mushroom to use for a head instead. I keep a pile of them near the front door to fling at the neighbor's ocelot, Sir Coughs-a-Lot. I don't HURT him; I just scare him away before he can get too close to me. Did I mention I don't like cats? Don't get me started. That's a whole other story.

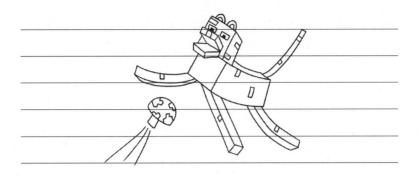

Anyway, the mushroom head didn't work and the golem DIDN'T come to life. (Big surprise there.) Cammy was so disappointed, her face got all red and scrunched up. Then she blew sky high, and it "snowed" gunpowder all over the yard.

For once, I was glad for the Exploding Baby's short fuse. See, after that, Mom was so busy trying to help Cammy pull herself together, she didn't notice when we sneaked into the house and back out again with the sled.

Sam and I had a BLAST on the snow hill. We stayed out all day, and I can barely keep my eyes open tonight. But now I'm well on my way to becoming the Overworld's greatest sledding creeper. And I'm only a couple of days into my 30-day plan!

DAY 3: SUNDAY (NIGHT)

I woke up again tonight to my sister's ugly mug, demanding her daily emeralds. And you know what I said? I said NO.

Just like that. NO.

I thought she might blow up right there on the spot, but instead she got this creepy smile on her face. She said she was just going to have to bring my sled into the kitchen to show Mom and Dad. "For your own good," she said, like she was doing me a favor by saving me from a life of crime or something.

"Go right ahead," I told her.

So she poked her head under the bed and came up red as an angry cave spider. "Where is it?" she demanded.

I told her that I took the sled back to the store. And got my money back.

"Well, if you have money, give me the emerald you owe me for today," she hissed.

And I said, "For what?"

"For not telling about the sled!" she almost shouted.

"WHAT sled?" I asked.

That time, she DID blow. Gunpowder floated down around us, and the water in Sticky's aquarium churned like a lava pit.

But you know what? It was WAY worth it, just seeing the look on my Evil Twin's face. Plus, I got to check something off my 30-day plan today.

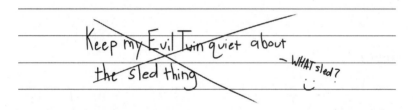

~~Keep my Evil Twin quiet about the sled thing~~ — WHAT sled? ☹

There's still a lot left on the list. I mean, I'm hoping Dad comes through for me on the job front, with something that doesn't require TOO much work. (I'm just a kid, after all.)

But it's only Day 3. I'll give the old man some more time.

DAY 4: MONDAY

So last night, I got the best idea for how to make more emeralds. I'd be swimming in them! It was all thanks to Ziggy Zombie—and believe me, THAT'S not something I say very often.

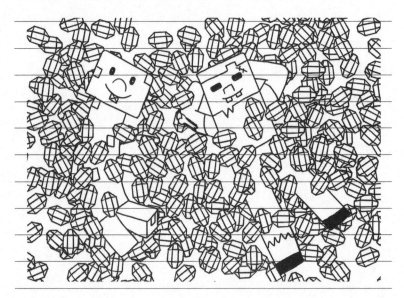

When we got to the sledding hill, Sam was acting all mopey. He said I wasn't giving him enough turns on the sled.

I almost pointed out that it was MY sled. But I guess he's kind of doing me a favor by hiding it from

Chloe, so I had to be nice. I said maybe we could try riding together on the sled. I already knew we wouldn't fit, but I thought I'd at least get points for offering.

When Sam shot that idea down, I had an even better one. I challenged him to a race down the hill. I said I'd ride the boring old sled and HE could slide down on his belly.

Sam actually thought that sounded pretty fun. And it WAS fun—until he started laughing. And jiggling. And hiccupping. And slid totally out of control. That slime's pretty fast, but he really needs to work on his steering.

He bounced a few times and then started to roll. By the time he reached the bottom of the hill, he looked like a ginormous snowball.

Did I mention that he crash-landed into someone's snow fort? Yeah, it wasn't pretty.

And for a second, I was SURE the fort belonged to Bones or some other spider jockey. Because that's the kind of thing that happens to Sam all the time— the slime's got really bad luck.

Turns out, it was Ziggy Zombie who crawled out! And he wasn't mad at all. People complain about zombies moaning and groaning about stuff, but Ziggy is actually pretty cheerful—at least when we let him hang out with us.

When Sam offered to help Ziggy fix his fort, he gave us a goofy green grin. And then we all got to work.

I thought re-building the snow fort was going to seriously cut into our sledding time, but then Willow Witch showed up. She'd been brewing a potion of swiftness, and she offered to share it with us so that we could build the fort even FASTER.

Well, my parents raised me right. I always say NO to stuff like that. Who knows what Willow puts in those potions? Spider eyes? Rabbit's feet? Ah, no, thank you.

But Sam and Ziggy each took a swig of potion from the bottle. And three minutes later, that fort was not only fixed, it was BIGGER than ever. Big enough for all of us to fit inside. So like I said, sometimes Willow Witch can be kinda cool.

We were all sitting in the fort when we got to talking about the holidays. Willow said her family was getting ready to celebrate the solstice, which is the shortest day of the year—and longest night. But this year, she said, solstice was going to fall on a school night. What a waste of extra time!

Ziggy said his family tradition was giving up eating rotten flesh for a week. I almost got up and did my happy dance when I heard that. No rotten flesh hanging from Ziggy's teeth for a WHOLE week? Now THAT was something to celebrate!

Sam started to talk about how his family lights torches every night for like eight nights in a row. But Ziggy interrupted him. He couldn't wait to tell us how HUMANS celebrate something called "Christmas" in the village.

See, Ziggy lives near a village and likes to stagger around at night, moaning and scaring villagers. It's a zombie thing, he says. And because of all that moaning and groaning, he knows more about humans than any of us do. So when he started to talk about Christmas, we all shut right up and listened.

Here's what Ziggy said about Christmas. (I don't know if I believe it all or not, but it SOUNDS kind of fun.)

- Some old, fat, jolly guy named Santa visits ALL the human kids in a single night and brings them presents. Yup, every last kid, Ziggy said. When I asked how

an old guy could get around the whole
Overworld in one night, Willow said maybe
he uses a potion of swiftness. I figure
that's a pretty good guess.

· Santa rides a sled pulled by critters called
reindeer. Ziggy says they're like horses
except they have these branches sticking
out of their heads. Oh, and they can fly.
(I'm not so sure about that last part. Ziggy
might have a few of his facts wrong.)

· Santa lands his sled on rooftops and comes down chimneys. Before I could ask Ziggy how, Willow said maybe Santa uses a potion of fire resistance so he doesn't get burned by the hot lava in the fireplace. (She's pretty smart. I can see why Sam likes her—not that I would EVER tell him that.)

· The kids hang stockings by the fireplace. It's how they get rid of old socks that don't match, Ziggy said. And then Santa puts little presents in them, like apples, to make them smell better.

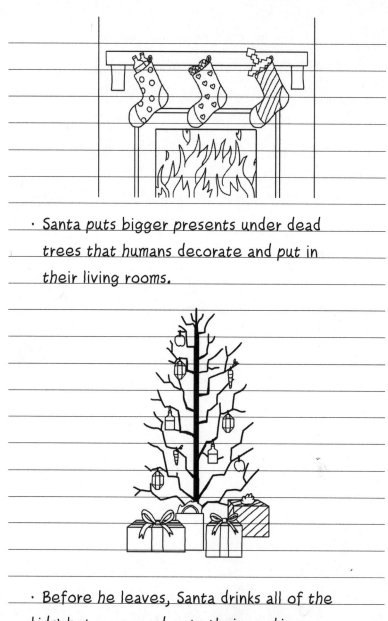

· Santa puts bigger presents under dead
trees that humans decorate and put in
their living rooms.

· Before he leaves, Santa drinks all of the
kids' hot cocoa and eats their cookies.

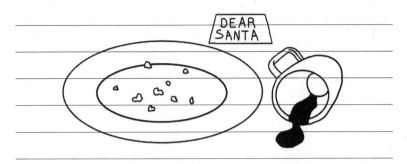

Willow _thought that_ was really mean, but then Ziggy said, "No! The kids love it when he comes!" He said that humans love Santa so much that they dress up like him. They wear padded suits and long white beards so that they look like the real Santa. And parents actually pay emeralds to have their kids sit on those fake Santas' laps.

Well, that's when I REALLY started paying attention. If I wanted to make a few emeralds, maybe all I had to do was dress up like this Santa dude.

I must have said that out loud, because Willow shot it down right away. She said there was NO WAY villager kids would believe I was Santa. She said they'd scream and run away from a green-faced Santa, like they do when they see zombies. "Right, Ziggy?" she asked.

He said she was right. But then he said baby ZOMBIES would LOVE to see a green-faced Santa—especially his baby sister, Zoe. And then Sam said his mini slime brothers would want to meet a green-faced Santa too.

"Would your parents pay emeralds?" I asked.

They both nodded. So . . .

BAM!

MASTER
PLAN

That's how it all started—my master plan for making emeralds to buy gifts for Creeper's Eve. We're going to have the Santa party for all the little mobs next Saturday.

I mean, the plan did change a little. I decided SAM should be the Santa, because he's pretty much the fattest and jolliest mob I know. And while he's entertaining all the baby mobs, I'll perform my new rap song. Did I mention I'm a rapper?

Willow wanted to know what my rap song was about. "What does it have to do with Santa?" she asked.

I told her it was ALL about Santa. But the truth was, I hadn't written it yet.

So that's why I'm staying up late this morning. If we're going to do the Santa party next weekend, I've got to get going on this rap. This is what I have so far:

Hey, hey, Kids, don't run away.

Santa's gonna come today!

Pay your emerald

Line up here

Whisper right in

Santa's ear. . .

Drool

Oops! Sorry about that.

I sort of fell asleep. Guess I'll write more tomorrow.

DAY 7: THURSDAY

Did I say I'd write more on Tuesday? Well, I couldn't, because I've been dealing with a LOT this week, let me tell you.

ALL my friends and I have done at school is fight about the Santa party.

I know, last time I wrote the party was really coming together. But let me catch you up on what's happened since then.

Monday night in math class, Ziggy and I disagreed about how much to charge for the party. Ziggy and I have never disagreed about ANYTHING—except about whether he should keep his mouth closed when he chews. (I sit by him at lunch, and it's totally disgusting.)

But on Monday, Ziggy said he thought I was charging too much for the Santa thing. Personally, I think he should leave the business stuff to me. He's not the brightest zombie in the pit. Plus, I think I had a pretty good plan. Here's what I was thinking:

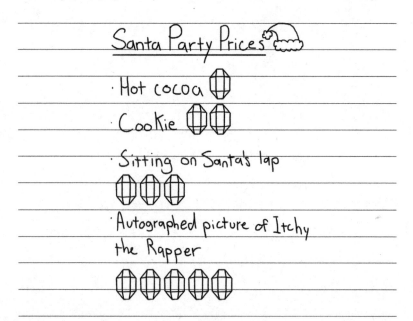

Santa Party Prices

· Hot cocoa
· Cookie
· Sitting on Santa's lap
· Autographed picture of Itchy the Rapper

Sounds good, right? But Ziggy didn't think so. Then our math teacher yelled at us for talking during class and separated us. Which was probably a good thing.

Then Tuesday night, at lunch, Willow said we should serve eggnog at the party. Egg WHAT? I didn't even know what that was. I figured it was one of her weird witches' brews. When she said the first ingredient was MILK, I immediately put the kibosh on the eggnog.

Why? Because my good buddy Sam is lactose intolerant. That means his body doesn't know what to do with milk. If he drinks it, his green belly bloats up with gas. And then? Bad things happen. REALLY bad things.

Yes, I'm sorry to say that I speak from experience. And let me tell you, the slime knows how to clear a room.

I tried to tell Willow about the lactose-intolerant thing, but for some reason, Sam kept interrupting me and changing the subject. So I guess he hasn't told Willow ALL his secrets yet.

Lucky for Sam, Eddy Enderman teleported into the lunchroom just then, and he kind of distracted me.

I was about to ask Eddy why we didn't see him on the sledding hill over the weekend. Most sixth-graders are afraid to talk to Eddy, because he's pretty much the coolest kid at school.

Plus, it's hard to talk to a mob when you can't look him in the eye.

But I know a few things about Eddy, just like I know a few things about Sam. Here's what I know:

- Eddy's real name is Louis—Louis Edward Enderman.
- His mom, Mrs. Enderwoman, is my history teacher. She's kind of strict, so I really try not to look HER in the eye.
- Eddy doesn't like rain or getting wet. (Now that I think about it, that's probably why he wasn't out sledding over the weekend.)

· If you look *him* in the eye, *he* WILL
teleport to you. But he's not looking to
pick a fight. He's too cool for that. He
just says stuff like, "What's up, dude?"
And sometimes, when I'm brave enough to
talk to him, he gives really good advice.

Anyway, the bell rang before I could talk to Eddy.
But by then, Sam and Willow were done talking
about eggnog. So I kind of missed my chance to
shoot that idea down.

Then, in the middle of art class, Sam and I got into
a fight about what kind of Christmas TREE to have at
the Santa party.

See, I thought we should decorate one of those
dead trees like the villagers do. I mean, if we're
going to do Christmas, we should do it right. Right?

But Sam thought we should decorate a CACTUS.
Because then it wouldn't have to be dead. He even
drew a picture of the cactus decorated in all these

twinkly lights. Our art teacher, Ms. Wanda, came by and gave him a compliment on it, which really didn't help matters.

See, I realized right then and there that I know all of Sam's secrets, but he doesn't know ME at all. If he did, he'd know that creepers and cactuses (cacti? cactis? cactusies?) are kind of like creepers and cats. We just don't get along.

~~Cacti~~

~~Cactis~~

~~Cactusies~~

Cactuses

How could Sam not KNOW that about me?

I didn't bother explaining it. But I decided to tell
Willow about Sam's little gas problem first chance I
get. Because I am NOT going to perform at a Santa
party with cactuses AND a stinky slime.

NO way.

DAY 9: SATURDAY

So just in case you were wondering, the party was an EPIC fail. And I blame Santa. Santa SAM, that is.

Do you know what that slime planned behind my back? Well, I guess Willow and ZIGGY knew the plan, because Ziggy could barely keep it to himself.

As soon as I got to the party, Ziggy said they had a surprise for me. He was grunting with excitement, and I could tell that the secret was gonna spill right out of his mouth like a hunk of rotten-flesh sandwich.

Willow could tell too, because she slapped her hand over his mouth. GROSS.

She wiped her hand on her robe afterward, but I hope she has zombie germs now. That would serve her right. You know why? Because she and her BOYFRIEND totally TRICKED me.

See, Sam bounced over all innocent-like and told me to close my eyes. Which I did. Partly because he looked so goofy in his Santa outfit, and I knew if I kept looking at him, I'd burst out laughing. And partly because I TRUSTED him.

HUGE mistake, that was.

He and Willow spun me in a circle, and when I opened my eyes, I was all wrapped up in twinkly lights. WHAT???

Then Sam announced that I was the Christmas tree for the party. "You didn't want a cactus tree, so we decided to have a CREEPER tree!" He laughed so hard, his whole body jiggled.

I _thought it_ was just one of Willow's dumb jokes. But as mobs and parents started showing up, I realized Sam and Willow were going to LEAVE me wrapped in those lights. ALL NIGHT. I was going to have to perform my RAP dressed like a talking, twinkling Christmas tree. And that's the kind of thing that can ruin a rapping career, let me tell you.

I ordered Sam to unwrap me PRONTO, but he completely ignored me. And as I watched him playing a jolly, jiggly Santa to baby zombies and sloppy mini slimes, my insides started bubbling like lava. I started to hiss. I ALMOST exploded right there on the spot (and I really try not to do that very often).

Then I saw that I was scaring one of the little zombies who was waiting in line to see Santa. It was Zoe, Ziggy's baby sister! I met her once at a sleepover. But now that I was all wrapped up like a Christmas tree, she didn't recognize me. (Go figure.)

I felt bad for scaring her. But when I saw her let a mini slime barge in line in front of her, I figured something out. She wasn't scared of ME. She was scared of SANTA.

So I crouched down next to her—which kind of hurts when you're wrapped up in twinkly lights. I asked her if she wanted to see Santa, and she shook her head. So I told her I was the Talking Tree and that she could talk to me instead of Santa, if she wanted to.

Slurp
Slurp
Slurp

She smiled and whispered something in my ear. Normally I don't let zombies get anywhere CLOSE to my face. But Zoe is a whole lot cuter than Ziggy— and not nearly as stinky and gross. (Too bad baby zombies have to grow up.)

Anyway, do you know what she said? She said Santa doesn't WIKE her. (Translation: Santa doesn't LIKE her. She was kind of slurping on her thumb.) She said he doesn't come see her because she's naughty and doesn't go to sleep.

Well, I don't know much about this Santa guy. But I think it's pretty unfair that village kids get to meet him and baby zombies don't. I told Zoe she wasn't naughty for staying awake.

"LOTS of kids stay awake," I said. "Like kids in the Nether. THEY don't sleep. And it's not because they're naughty. It's because they don't have beds. Do you know what happens to beds in the Nether?"

Zoe's eyes got wide and she shook her head.

"They blow up!" I whispered.

"So there's no sleeping in the Nether." I made a funny face, and Zoe giggled. I thought I handled that one pretty well. Turns out, I was kind of a natural at this Talking Tree thing.

Before Zoe ran back to her parents, she handed me a crumpled-up piece of paper. It was a drawing of a tiny green blob next to a big red blob. Someone, maybe Ziggy, had written "Zoe" under the green blob and "Santa" under the red one.

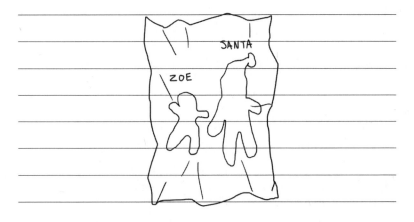

But Zoe didn't give it to Santa. She gave it to ME.

Well, I had to admit, that was pretty cute. I didn't even mind that the paper was probably full of zombie germs. I smoothed it out and stuck it under the row of twinkly lights that was stretched across my stomach like a belt.

But by the time I stood back up, the line of kids in front of Sam was GONE. Parents were leaving— RUNNING for the door, actually. And I hadn't even done my rap!

What in the Overworld was going on???

That's when I saw Santa Sam, sitting in the middle of a GINORMOUS green cloud, holding a cup of eggnog. Looking like he'd just ruined Christmas.

GREAT.

I couldn't get out of that room fast enough. I mean, it's pretty much impossible to run when your legs are wrapped in twinkly lights. Plus, I almost slipped on a mini slime on my way out the door.

So like I said, the party was a total disaster. We earned a few emeralds. But after Sam and I split them, there were barely enough left over to pay Willow back for the eggnog ingredients. I bet she'll never make THAT again.

Anyway, I keep looking at the picture Zoe made of Santa. And I'm thinking, this Santa guy sure has a lot of work to do. Maybe TOO much work, because he's kind of blowing it. The dude needs some help.

So now I'm wondering . . . Is there a way for ME to help him out? And to earn more emeralds at the same time? And to make Santa WIKE Zoe and maybe visit her once in a while?

I guess I need to add one more thing to my 30-day plan. I swear, that list is getting longer instead of shorter. But this one's important.

· Help out Santa. (And the baby zombie.)

DAY 11: MONDAY

Man, this creeper can't catch a break.

Last night, Sam and I were sledding. Yeah, I know,
I should be mad at him for turning me into a Talking
Tree. But Sam's kind of got me in a trap, because
he still has my sled. And there's still snow on the
ground. So . . .

I met him at the hill and pretended like everything
was cool. But it STOPPED being cool when Chloe
showed up.

Let me back up for a sec. You know how Mom has been all about family time lately? Well, she keeps coming up with these new family traditions. And I think she's getting ideas from all the wrong people.

At dinner, she decided that our "tradition of the day" would be to get a Christmas tree. SERIOUSLY??? It's like all the Christmas trees of the Overworld have turned against me and decided to make my life miserable.

I still have lines on my face from the twinkly lights wrapped around my head the other night, so the LAST thing I want to see in our living room is one of those dead trees. ~~I'd almost rather see a CACTUS there.~~ (Wait, scratch that. I didn't really mean it.)

Anyway, when Mom invited us all to go get a tree together, I told her I couldn't. "I have important holiday business to take care of," I fibbed.

Mom actually smiled at that. Maybe she thought I was going shopping for gifts for the family. And that counted as "family time," so she let me off the hook. (I'll have to remember that excuse for later. It's a keeper.)

But I'd only taken one turn on the sled before Chloe showed up. Mom, Cate, and Cammy were right behind her, lugging a really big spruce tree across the snow. Dad was nowhere in sight, so I figured he must have sneaked off for some "business" of his own. Have I mentioned Dad is a master sneaker-offer?

Anyway, when Chloe saw me standing by the sled, she shouted, "Hey, whose sled is that?"

Sam was just getting onto the sled. He was about to tell her EXACTLY who owned the sled. "Ger—" he started to say.

That was when I gave the sled a little nudge with my foot, just to help him along. As he took off down the hill with a surprised look on his jiggly green face, I finished his word for him. "Ger . . . onimo!"

Then I turned to Chloe and said, "It's Sam's sled. Obviously."

But she narrowed her eyes. She KNEW. And when I got home this morning, she busted me.

"You didn't return the s-s-sled to the s-s-store," she hissed. "Your s-s-slimy friend S-S-Sam is HIDING it for you. And I'm going to tell Mom." Then she cocked her creeper head. "Unlessss . . ."

She was working up to another bribe, I could tell. So I told her right away I didn't have any more emeralds. That wasn't totally true. But I wasn't

about to give the emeralds I'd earned as a Talking
Tree to my Evil Twin. No way, no how.

"Unless . . ." she said again, "you and Sam give me a
ride to school every night. On that sled."

I blew out my breath and stared at her. Was she
bluffing? Usually, Chloe didn't want anything to do
with me at school. She didn't even want other mobs
to know we were related. So maybe this was just a
threat and she wouldn't follow through.

"Whatever," I grumbled. I pretended to give in so
that she would just GO AWAY. And she did.

I don't know yet if I'm going to have to drag my sister to school on that sled, but I do know this: the one thing I thought I'd checked off my 30-Day Plan is now back on.

· Keep my Evil Twin quiet about sled thing

"One step forward, two steps back," Dad likes to say. I never knew what he meant by that. But this morning, I know EXACTLY what he means.

DAY 12: TUESDAY

Sometimes a night starts out one way and ends up a whole different way.

Last night started out TERRIBLE. Yeah, it really stunk. Chloe decided she did want that ride to school, so Sam showed up with the sled after dinner.

But Chloe was HEAVY. Especially when we were pulling her uphill. Was that girl hiding blocks of obsidian in her shoes or what?

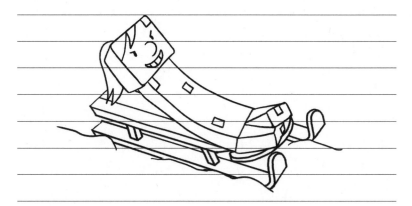

I made Sam help me pull. I figured since we were sharing ownership of the sled, we should share the work too. (I mean, it's only fair.)

But Chloe treated us like a couple of horses. "Faster!" she kept saying.

Then Bones and his gang showed up, like they always do at the WORST possible times. Bones pulled a carrot out of his backpack and stuck it in front of our noses. I didn't know what was up with that—until he started SNORTING.

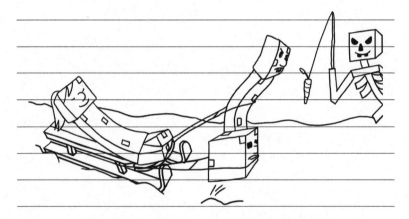

"Oink, oink, little piggies," he said, as if we were a couple of those pigs you can tame with a carrot on a fishing rod. GREAT.

Well, that pretty much did it. Bones's bony buddies started OINKing and SNORTing too. Which meant that

every kid we passed stopped and stared. Every.
Single. One.

So you know, if you ever want to REALLY draw
attention to yourself, I can give you a few pointers.

But it all ended the second that Bones and his
buddies turned on Chloe.

See, my Evil Twin can dish out the insults, but she
sure can't take them. All Bones had to do was call
her a Zombie Pig Girl.

Well, I've been called WAY worse than that. But Chloe's green skin must be really thin. She blew sky high before Bones was even done laughing. It was like, "Bah, ha, ha—"

BOOM!!!

Luckily, Chloe had rolled off the sled by then. And the girl DOES know how to make a dramatic exit. Bones and his buddies got blown back a few feet, and Sam and I made our getaway in a cloud of gunpowder.

I thought we'd have to go through the whole thing again on the way HOME from school, but like I said, sometimes nights have a way of turning around.

See, for starters, Chloe had to go to Strategic Explosions class after school, so we didn't have to worry about dragging her highness, the Zombie Pig Princess, back home.

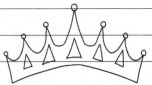

The sled felt a THOUSAND tons lighter without her, even with our backpacks piled onto it. And we were making pretty good time back to Sam's house.

Then Willow showed up and cracked some dumb joke, like, "Hey, if it isn't Santa and his sleigh!" Sam laughed his slimy green head off at that, acting like it was WAY funnier than it was. (Sometimes I swear Willow is using a love potion on him or something.)

But her dumb little joke reminded me of something. It reminded me of Zoe's puny green face, asking why Santa never came to see her.

So I told Sam and Willow what I'd been thinking. I told them about how there were all these little mobs who didn't get a visit from Santa on Christmas. And how unfair that was. And how maybe we could HELP Santa do a better job—and hey, maybe even make a few emeralds doing it!

"You could wear my Santa suit," Sam offered. Which I guess meant he was done being Santa, and I was on my own this time.

Well, I've SEEN his Santa suit, and you could fit about twelve of me in it.

So I told him that my sister Cate, the Fashion Queen, could probably whip up some kind of Santa suit for me from all the things in her messy closet.

"But do you think parents would PAY to have Santa visit their kids on Christmas?" I asked Sam and Willow. I really wanted to know if my plan could work.

Sam nodded his wiggly head up and down so hard, he almost fell over. "I'd pay emeralds for Santa to come visit my little brothers," he said.

"Really?" I asked. "Would you pay EIGHTEEN emeralds? Six for each brother?" I don't know where that number even came from. I guess numbers and business stuff just come easy for me. Kind of like rap songs.

Sam said he didn't know—that he'd sure have to do a lot of babysitting to earn that many emeralds. But he said he'd try.

Willow said she knew a witch with FIVE little sisters, and that she would ask her about a Santa visit. "But no promises," she said.

By then, we'd caught up to Ziggy Zombie. (Zombies aren't exactly known for their speed.) And when we told him the plan, he said he was pretty sure he could come up with six emeralds for me to come visit Zoe.

WOO-HOO!

My head was spinning with emeralds all night long. I couldn't concentrate in class, and I could barely eat at lunchtime.

(And it wasn't just because Ziggy's rotten-flesh fajitas stunk up the whole lunchroom.)

At this rate, I figured I'd have enough emeralds to buy gifts for my family. Enough emeralds to keep Chloe quiet for FOREVER about the sled. (Or, at least, until after Creeper's Eve.) Oh, and even enough emeralds to buy fireworks for ME for the new year.

So like I said, the night started off pretty rough. But Mom says when life hands you mushrooms, you should make mushroom stew.

And let me tell you, I can smell that stew already.

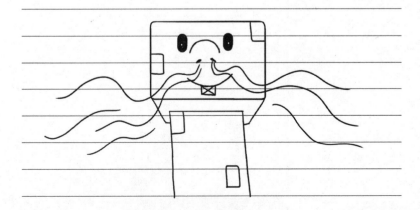

DAY 13: WEDNESDAY

Here's why I think Santa works alone: because Santa's helpers have ROTTEN ideas.

When I walked home from school with my friends this morning, I was talking about what kinds of things to put in the little mobs' socks on Christmas. Ziggy reminded me they were called STOCKINGS. Whatever—that's not the important part.

What's important is what I'm going to stuff inside the stinky socks. And it can't be something that costs emeralds, because I'm trying to EARN those, not spend a bunch of them. That's just not good business.

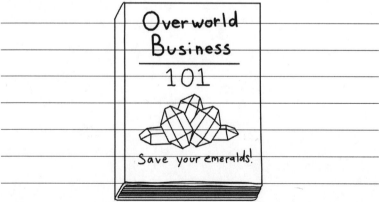

Overworld
Business
101

Save your emeralds!

So I asked my friends what they thought about gunpowder. I mean, we have a whole trash can full of it in the garage from all of Cammy's explosions. So it wouldn't cost me any emeralds. And, hey, the little mobs could make fireworks with it!

I was sure at least one of my friends would cheer or tell me how great my idea was. But even Sam stayed quiet. Maybe it was because I was making him pull the sled home, and he was still tired from pulling Chloe to school.

Instead of backing up my idea, Willow had to point out that fireworks aren't SAFE for little mobs.

Who blew up and made her the teacher around here?

Anyway, she said she had a better idea. Wanna know what it was? (Trust me, you really don't.)

Willow's great idea was SPIDER EYES. Sometimes I wonder if that girl is high on her own potions or something.

I tried to tell her that no kid wants to reach into a stocking and pull out a slimy spider eye.

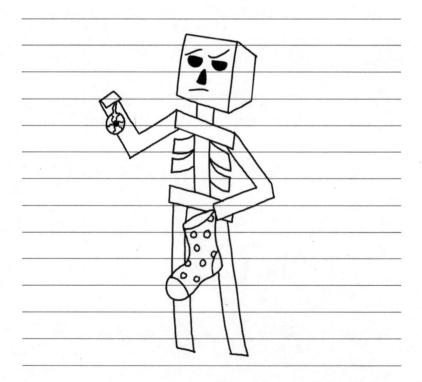

Ziggy backed me up on that one, which I thought was pretty decent of him. But then he suggested I put rotten FLESH in the stockings. So I don't know where he gets off shooting down spider eyes.

I was hoping Sam would save the day and vote for gunpowder. Instead, he suggested slimeballs. So now you see what I mean about Santa's helpers. Who needs 'em?

When we couldn't agree on stocking stuffers, Ziggy asked why I didn't just do what the real Santa does and put apples in the stockings.

I reminded him that I don't have an apple tree in my backyard. And if I did, it would be frozen solid right now. And a bag of apples costs like five emeralds or something at the store. So there.

Then Willow said, "Doesn't your mom buy apples?"

I'm pretty sure I rolled my eyes. Sometimes I think my friends don't know me at all.

"Creepers aren't big on fruits and vegetables," I told her.

Then I remembered that wasn't TOTALLY true. Mom was on this "going green" kick for a while when all she served for breakfast and dinner was green vegetables. I really don't like to think about that time, because I had a pretty bad experience with brussels sprouts.

Also, Mom does make apple crisp sometimes. But she burns it to an extra crispy crisp so we don't have to taste the apples. (And I really appreciate that about her cooking.)

So that got me to thinking. If I could convince Mom that apples were GOOD for us, like those brussels sprouts, maybe she would buy them more often. And then I could sneak off with a couple every day until I had enough for Christmas.

GENIUS!

Like I said, who needs helpers? I'm a Santa with a plan.

DAY 15: FRIDAY

I blew up two houses with one explosion last night.
(Not really. It's just an expression.)

See, I managed to talk my mom into buying apples
AND talk my sister into making me a Santa suit. All in
one conversation.

I started out by telling Mom how much I loved
dinner. That part was true, because she'd made pork
chops and roasted potatoes—my FAVORITE. I might
have gone kind of overboard, because my Evil Twin
pretended to be throwing up behind Mom's back.
But I ignored her and kept talking.

You're so sweet, Gerald!

I told Mom how the only thing that would make dinner even BETTER would be one of her famous burnt apple crisps. And then I told her all kinds of interesting facts about apples that I'd researched at school on Thursday night:

- Apples used to be really rare in the Overworld. You could only find them in dungeon chests. So we should be GRATEFUL to be able to buy them in the supermarket. And we should show our gratitude by buying MORE.

- Villagers like to trade for apples— sometimes even for emeralds! So having apples is ALMOST like having emeralds. It's like a savings account.

Cha Ching!

81

· Right after you eat an apple, you can
walk through fire. Willow told me that
one. It's true—honest! But only if the
apple is golden. And enchanted. Mom
doesn't have to know ALL those details,
though.

Mom was nodding and smiling and going right along
with my plan. Then she launched a surprise attack.
She said, "Maybe we should eat fewer pork chops
and potatoes around here and eat more apples!"

UH-OH. Leave it to Mom to take things WAY too far.

I had to squash that idea like a silverfish—FAST.

I started babbling something about how apples
taste best when they come AFTER pork chops. I
said that pork chops and apples go together like
chickens and eggs. Mooshrooms and milk. Rotten
flesh and—

WHAT? Where did THAT come from? I blame Ziggy
Zombie for putting those two words in my head and
almost ruining my plan.

Dad must have seen me struggling, because he
cleared his throat and said the perfect thing. He
said that maybe we should ALL make apple crisp
together, as a family. Mom could teach us!

Well, I could have kissed Gerald Creeper Senior—if
creeper sons did that kind of thing, I mean. I guess
Dad has more experience with Mom and knows how
to put the kibosh on her big ideas (at least the
ones that have to do with pork chops). He saved MY
creeper butt, that's for sure.

Mom ate Dad's idea right up. She said she'd buy a bag of apples at the store right away. TWO bags of apples. Maybe even three!

So that meant I could check "apples" off my list and move on to the NEXT part of my plan.

I mentioned kind of cool and casual-like that apple-red was my new favorite color.

That's not true AT ALL. Everybody knows my favorite color is green. And my Evil Twin was the first one to call me out on it—which was exactly what I wanted her to do.

She said, "You don't like red. Show me one red thing in your room."

Then I said, "Actually, I was thinking about wearing more red. In fact, I think it'd be cool to wear a whole SUIT out of red, like that Santa guy the villager kids talk about. If only I knew someone who had a bunch of extra wigs and skins . . ."

See what I did there?

Well, Cate just about fell out of her chair offering to help.

She said she'd check her closet for me right now, before school. In fact, she invited me to go WITH her to her closet.

I had to think about that for a second. Cate's closet is kind of like the Nether. You can get into it, but you probably won't find your way out. A creeper could get lost and starve to death in there, for sure.

So I almost said I'd wait in the kitchen and let Cate go on ahead. But Mom was close to exploding with happiness, seeing me bond with one of my sisters. So I decided to take one for the team and go with Cate.

Boy, was I glad I did. I went in looking like plain old Gerald Creeper Jr., and I came out looking like a jolly green Santa. All it took was:

· A long red velvet bathrobe. (Do NOT tell anyone I'm wearing a girl's robe.)

· A red purse that we turned upside down
to make a hat. (I prefer to call it a
"pouch," not a purse. But whatever.)

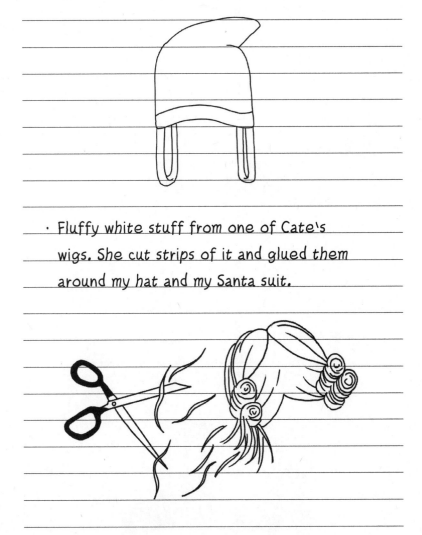

· Fluffy white stuff from one of Cate's
wigs. She cut strips of it and glued them
around my hat and my Santa suit.

· A black belt with a shiny buckle. (It's kind of tight, but I'm sure it'll fit better after I've digested my pork chops.)

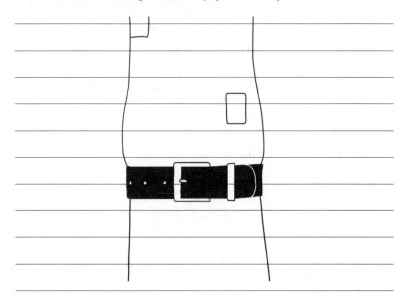

· Black boots. The heels are kind of high, but by the time we got down to the boots, I was ready to be done with the whole closet dress-up thing.

When Cate said she still had to put white makeup on my face, I made a run for it—which was NOT easy in those high-heeled boots.

But now the Santa suit is safely hidden under my bed, where the sled used to be. And I'm going to borrow Cate's glue to put my piggy bank back together, because pretty soon, it's going to be chock FULL of emeralds.

DAY 16: SATURDAY

So last night, I walked to school with Sam. Pulling my sled. With my Evil Twin stretched out on it. She had a super-smug smile on her face that I wanted to wipe off with a snowball.

At least I've got Sam pulling the sled by himself now. I told him what good exercise it is. And I pointed out a few muscles in his wiggly back that I hadn't noticed before, which made him pretty happy.

So after Chloe hopped off, we met up with Willow. And when Sam saw her, he started flexing his muscles and stuff. I think he was trying to look tough, but he just looked like he had to pee.

That was when Eddy Enderman teleported to us out of NOWHERE. I almost jumped, but I tried to play it cool.

"Ah, hey, Eddy," I said.

And he was like, "Hey, Gerald. What's with the sled?"

I wasn't sure how to answer that. I mean, Eddy's not big on snow. So I didn't want to talk up my sled like it was the best thing ever. Even though it kind of is.

Before I could answer, my big-mouthed best friend answered for me. "He's going to play Santa and use the sled as a sleigh."

Well, I almost blew up with embarrassment right then and there. PLAY Santa, he said. Like I was some little kid or something! I REALLY couldn't look Eddy in the eye after that.

But this is why Eddy is the coolest kid ever.

He didn't make me feel dumb about the Santa thing.
Instead, he asked a very good question—a question
that I hadn't even thought of yet.

CRUD.

No, I told him, I did not have any reindeer yet.

And then he kind of shrugged. At least I think he
did, but since I was staring at his legs, I couldn't say

for sure. Then he told me that he had a wolf that liked to pull sleds. "You can borrow her if you want," he said.

And then he was gone.

Willow and Sam stared at me like I'd just taken down an Ender Dragon or something.

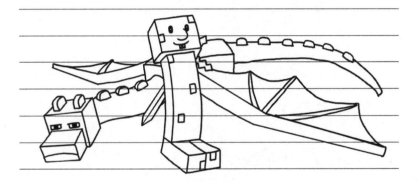

"Did Eddy Enderman REALLY just offer you his wolf to pull your sled?" asked Willow.

Now it was my turn to play it cool. I just shrugged and said, "Yeah. No biggie. We're friends."

But inside? I felt like I was going to blow sky high.

With JOY.

And now that I'm home, I can't even THINK about going to sleep. So I've been counting sheep. And reindeer. And reindeer-wolves.

Now that my plan is rolling forward, Christmas can't come soon enough!

DAY 17: SUNDAY

So I invited myself to Ziggy Zombie's for a
sleepover last night. I really try to avoid those
kinds of things, because hanging out with Ziggy at
school is WAY more than enough.

But I needed to scope out the joint—er, his house.
I had to figure out a plan for coming down his
chimney and stuff. I mean, Christmas is only ONE
week away! And now that I've got a suit, a sled, and
a reindeer-wolf, I'm starting to take my job as Fake
Santa pretty seriously.

Right away, Ziggy wanted me to listen to his new
"Moans and Groans" playlist. That's not really my
kind of music, but I didn't figure Ziggy had a lot of
rap in his collection. So I said sure, as long we could
listen to it in the living room.

Pretty soon he was dancing to the music—if you can
call it that. Mostly he just staggered around the
living room with a goofy grin on his face.

That gave me time to check out the fireplace. And do you know what I saw crawling out of that thing? A HUGE HAIRY SPIDER.

Yup, I almost screeched like a ghast in the Nether.

Until I saw that it was LEGGY, Ziggy's pet spider.

I'm not a big fan of Leggy. See, he spins these
webs all over the place, and for some reason, I
ALWAYS get stuck in them. So sharing the chimney
with Leggy is just not going to work for me on
Christmas.

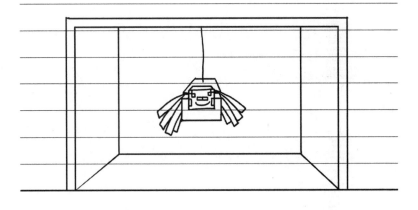

I told Ziggy that. He had to turn down his music
to hear me, but he said he knew JUST how to keep
Leggy out of the chimney.

Then the zombie poured a bucket of lava into the
fireplace. As if FLAMES shooting up the chimney

was going to make it easier for me to come down. Sometimes I think that zombie has a head full of rotten flesh instead of brains.

Then I remembered what Willow said about potion of fire resistance. Could she brew me up some of that stuff? I didn't have a lot of time to think about it, because Zoe suddenly zoomed into the living room, riding her pet chicken.

Why can't zombies have NORMAL pets, like squids?

Anyway, Zoe was so FAST on that chicken—like a tiny spider jockey. But she kept getting too close to the lava in the fireplace. Ziggy told her to slow down, but she listened to him about as much as my sisters listen to me. Which is not a lot.

Then Ziggy said if *she* stopped riding around like a crazy zombie, he'd tell her a secret.

I *thought that was a GREAT idea, until I heard what* he said. (Zombies really don't know how to whisper.)

SANTA IS GOING TO COME VISIT YOU THIS YEAR!

After he told Zoe the big secret—MY big secret— he grinned at me and tried to wink. Or maybe he just had a twitch in his eyebrow.

Either way, I did NOT smile back. Partly because I had just gotten stuck in one of Leggy's cobwebs, and partly because now that Zoe knows Santa is coming, there's no backing out.

Not even if the chimney is full of cobwebs.

Or shooting flames of lava sky high.

I'm in this thing now. And there's no turning back.

DAY 19: TUESDAY

You know, you just don't know what you've got 'til it's gone.

That's what Cate said after Dad made her break up with her boyfriend Steve. I'm not really sure she ever HAD Steve. See, he was human and a miner.

And everyone knows that miners and mobs don't mix. (Plus, I saw him hanging out with some redheaded girl in the village once, but that's a whole other story.)

See, I THOUGHT I had a plan for Christmas. I had my Santa suit. I scoped out at least one chimney. And last night, I even talked Willow into brewing me a potion of fire resistance. I'm not crazy about drinking something with a bunch of slimy magma cream in it, believe me. But a Santa's got to do what a Santa's got to do.

But this whole time, there was one thing I kind of took for granted. (That means you don't really appreciate it while you have it.)

SNOW.

Yup, the white stuff that hit me in the forehead eighteen days ago is starting to MELT. And what's Santa without snow?

Boy, I did NOT see this coming. Someone really should have warned me.

It was almost IMPOSSIBLE to pull Chloe to school on the sled last night. At least, that's what Sam said when he finally gave up and plopped down onto his butt on the grass.

Chloe got mad at first, but when she saw that he wasn't getting up, she finally crept off in a hissy huff. She said she'd have to come up with something ELSE we could do for her.

But I can't worry about that right now. Because without snow, I can't use my sled on Christmas. And it's only SIX days away!

What is this Santa supposed to do? WALK from house to house? Ride Eddy's wolf? Bounce across the plains on Sam?

Santa's Ride???

I actually *thought* about that last idea for a while. But then I *thought* of all *the* ways Sam could wreck my plan. He'd probably want to come down the chimney with me, and that slime would get stuck for sure.

He'd probably drink all *the* hot chocolate the kids left for Santa, and then he'd have a gas attack before we could make it back up the chimney.

Yeah, Sam would give Santa a bad name. Kids would be holding their noses and begging him NOT to come back next year.

And that would be the end of my new career.

So . . . I decided to go with a different approach.

Dad once told me that ancient humans used to do "rain dances" to make it rain here in the Overworld. When I asked if that actually worked, Dad said he wasn't so sure.

Well, that was a good enough answer for me. I decided to try a SNOW dance. What does this creeper have to lose?

This morning after school, I crept outside while my family was sleeping. I stood under the rising sun and started moving and grooving. Let me tell you, I boogied my butt off. I did every single dance move I could think of, and that was A LOT:

· I tried out some of Mom's Zombie Zumba.

· I pulled out my best hip-hop. (When a rabbit went by, I even squatted down and bunny-hopped.)

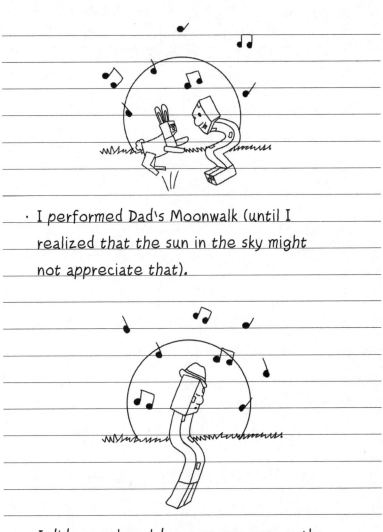

· I performed Dad's Moonwalk (until I
realized that the sun in the sky might
not appreciate that).

· I did some breakdance moves across the
porch. (Actually, the only thing I BROKE
was one of Mom's flowerpots, but my
landing was pretty impressive.)

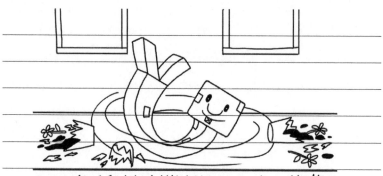

I was hurting after that crash landing—I'm not gonna lie. But I got up anyway and did the Stanky Legg with my one GOOD leg.

And the whole time I was dancing, I stared at the sky and hoped for another miracle.

But nothing came down. Nothing except a couple of crumbly dead leaves that I must have bumped loose from the roof with all that dancing. And the forecast called for sunny skies ahead.

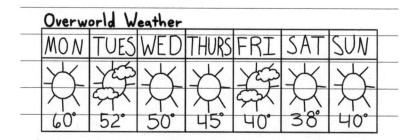

Overworld Weather

MON	TUES	WED	THURS	FRI	SAT	SUN
60°	52°	50°	45°	40°	38°	40°

Did I do the wrong dance? Who knows. It's not like I can check out a book on "Snow Dancing" from the school library.

But if this dancing thing doesn't pay off, I'm going to have to figure out something else. FAST.

DAY 21: THURSDAY

Did I mention that I'm running out of time?

"Don't panic, Gerald," I keep telling myself. "Keep it together, dude."

But that's hard to do when Christmas is creeping closer. And there's still NO SNOW on the ground. In fact, the grass is as green as a slime on a sunny day. It's SO annoying!

I'm starting to think I have to give up on the sled thing and find another way for Santa Gerald to travel. I could really use some time to THINK about that. But Mom's decided that we're going to make a different kind of apple dessert every night. As a family. Before school. Which seriously cuts into my thinking time.

And really, how many different kinds of apple dessert can there be? I made the mistake of asking

Mom that, and she started listing them off. Which
just ate up more time. Big mistake.

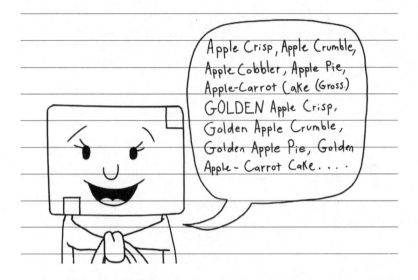

> Apple Crisp, Apple Crumble,
> Apple Cobbler, Apple Pie,
> Apple-Carrot Cake (Gross.)
> GOLDEN Apple Crisp,
> Golden Apple Crumble,
> Golden Apple Pie, Golden
> Apple-Carrot Cake. . . .

Plus, Chloe has decided that since Sam and I can't
pull her to school on a sled anymore, I should pay
for her silence in a different way—by doing her
MATH homework every morning when we get home.

At first, I thought that would be a cinch. See, I'm
a whiz at math, and Chloe, well, isn't. But then I
realized that if Chloe started turning in GOOD work,
her teacher would know right away she was cheating
and probably bust us both. So I'd have to do BAD or

so-so work, and that was going to take a lot more time.

I fumed about that while I stole a few apples to save for kids' stockings. I had just stuffed the apples under my itchy wool sweater and was creeping back to my room.

And I really *hoped* Chloe wouldn't see me, because the last thing I needed was for her to bust me doing TWO sneaky things.

Instead—and this was the best part of my whole day—I busted HER doing something, or at least planning something.

See, her friend Cora Creeper had just shown up
to walk to school with her, and they were talking
in Chloe's room. I heard Cora say something about
"scoring a new, faster ride to school," and then
Chloe hushed Cora, and they both started laughing.
Well, I'm no dummy. It was the hushing and the
laughing that kind of clued me in. Chloe was UP to
something.

Dad always says that two wrongs don't make a right.
But I got to thinking—if CHLOE did something wrong
and got busted, then maybe HER wrong would cancel

out MY wrong. And she wouldn't be able to hold the sled thing over my head anymore.

$$f(x) = \frac{2x}{\pi} - \left(\frac{\pi}{4}\right) \Big| + \frac{6x}{3\pi} \cos\left(\frac{n^2}{5}\right)$$

$$= \frac{-4}{n} \sin\left(\frac{\pi}{6}\right) \Big|_0^2 + \frac{9x}{n^2} \cos\left(\frac{\pi}{2}\right) \Big|_0^2$$

$$\left[\frac{2}{\pi} \cos(\pi)\left(\frac{9}{6}\right) + \frac{3}{n^2}\right] = \left(\frac{4^2}{6}\right)\Big|_0^2 + 5$$

GERALD BUSTED + CHLOE BUSTED

= GERALD NOT BUSTED

Like I said, I'm pretty good at math—maybe even better than Dad.

So I'm going to keep an eye on my Evil Twin, night and day. If she's doing something wrong, I'll bust her.

Plus, I gotta say, I'm kind of interested in this faster ride to school. Because this fake Santa NEEDS a fast ride, now that my sled is gathering dust in the garage.

Did I mention I'm running out of time???

FOUR days 'til Christmas.

And counting . . .

DAY 22: FRIDAY

Chloe was sure in a hurry to leave school this morning. She pretty much threw her backpack at me, told me to do a good job on her math homework (translation: do a BAD job, like she would), and then took off toward the minefields. Why wasn't she going to Strategic Explosions class?

Then it hit me. This was IT—Chloe was about to do something sketchy. And I wasn't gonna miss the chance to bust her doing it. No, sirree.

I made Sam come with me, because every good detective needs a sidekick. Plus he'd be the perfect witness for Chloe's evil doings. Sam would tell my parents exactly what he saw, and everyone KNOWS Sam can't tell a lie.

OK, OK! I'll tell you everything!

But then Willow ended up coming too, because she and Sam are *pretty much* joined at the hip. (BARF.) I hoped she at least had a potion of invisibility or something in her backpack.

By the time we got to the minefields, we couldn't see Chloe anywhere. But when we crept toward the nearest cave, I could HEAR her voice coming from inside.

I'd know *that* voice anywhere. (It's the second most annoying sound ever. The only WORSE sound is Ziggy Zombie smacking on his flesh sandwiches. EWW.)

Then we heard something else—the screech of a cave spider. Now if you ever tell anyone this, I will deny it. And I'll never write another word in this notebook again. But here's the truth: I was so scared that I ALMOST blew up. The only reason I didn't is because Sam pretty much jumped into Willow's arms.

And that made me laugh. And the only creeper who can laugh and blow up at the same time is Cammy, the Exploding Baby.

Sam almost knocked Willow over, and then he was so embarrassed, I thought he'd melt into a million mini slimes.

But when we saw what was making the sound, we all forgot about Sam's moment of shame.

See, it wasn't a spider at all. It was a MINECART squeaking and squealing on rusty wheels. Chloe and Cora and a few other creepers pushed that old minecart right out of the cave.

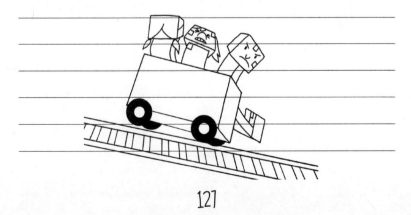

Was THAT Chloe's new, faster ride? It looked like it was going to break into a gazillion pieces. But it didn't. They pushed that cart all the way to school and then hid it in the trees by the sledding hill.

After Chloe headed home, my friends and I got a closer look at that minecart. And I knew they were thinking the same thing I was, because pretty soon Willow asked, "Do you think Eddy Enderman's wolf-dog could pull this cart?"

Yup, I do think so.

And I'm going to ask Eddy tonight at school, first chance I get.

DAY 24: SUNDAY (MORNING)

Ziggy says that tonight is what's called "Christmas Eve." He said human kids are nervous on Christmas Eve because they know Santa is coming. Well, I'm here to tell you, SANTA gets nervous too. My insides are all fizzy and sloshing around, like one of Willow's potions.

Maybe it's because Eddy Enderman met me at the sledding hill this morning with his wolf-dog, Pearl. And I don't think she likes me very much. She sniffed one of my green feet, and just when I thought she was going to lick it, she GROWLED instead.

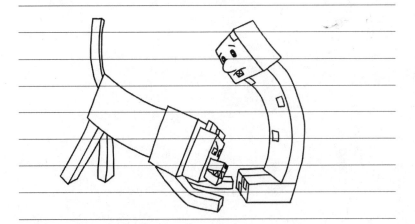

Eddy said not to worry—that if I feed her enough skeleton bones, she'll do whatever I want. I ALMOST asked him where he got those skeleton bones, but I didn't. I just tried not to think about it as he showed me how to put on Pearl's harness.

Luckily, Chloe and her friends hadn't moved the minecart from its hiding spot. Maybe it was because they couldn't figure out how to pull it. I mean, not everyone is friends with an Enderman with a sled-pulling wolf-dog, right?

Anyway, pretty soon, I was sitting next to Eddy in that old minecart, which could have been a pretty cool moment—if I weren't having a TOTAL FREAKOUT.

Because driving that minecraft sleigh was a whole lot harder than it looked!

If I tugged the reins attached to Pearl's harness to the right, she would SORT of go right. But she wasn't big on going left. Which meant I'd probably just end up riding around in circles on Christmas Day.

Eddy hung out with me as long as he could, but when the sun started to come up, he hopped out of the cart and was by Pearl's side in flash. "See ya tonight, Gerald," he said as he grabbed Pearl's collar and teleported away.

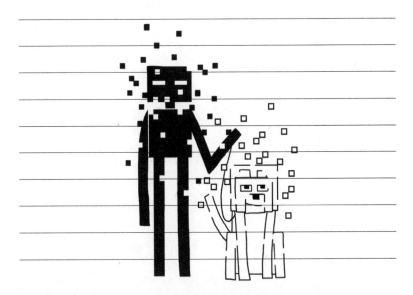

Then it was just me sitting in that minecart, wondering what in the Overworld I was getting myself into.

Twenty-four hours 'til Christmas. And counting . . .

DAY 24: SUNDAY (NIGHT)

You know what? If I could ask the real Santa for one Christmas wish, I'd wish for new FRIENDS. Because mine really STINK!!!

I don't even know where to start. Every time I try to write about it, my insides boil up and start to fizz over. I haven't blown up yet, but if Sam apologizes even ONE more time, I will, I swear.

It was all in place. Every. Last. Detail.

I got dressed in that dumb Santa suit, right down to the high-heeled boots that made it hard to creep ANYWHERE without making a bunch of noise. And I turned my itchy wool sweater into a sack for carrying apples.

Then my friends came over so we could plan my route—you know, like which house to go to first. I asked my friends to pay up the emeralds they owed me, because I'd finally glued my piggy bank back together. And everyone KNOWS you don't deliver goods until your customers pay up.

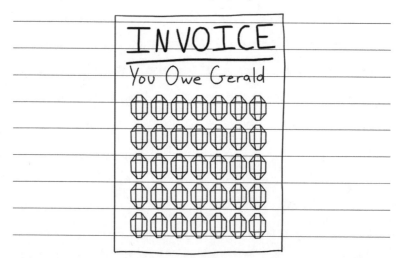

Well, that's when the WHOLE thing fell apart.

Sam said that he'd been so busy pulling my sister around to school, he hadn't really had time to babysit his brothers. So he didn't QUITE have the eighteen emeralds he owed me.

Well, I said, NO problem. I'd take half now and half later. That's the kind of friend I am.

And you know what he said? He said he didn't have half. And when I got up in his face about it, he said he didn't have ANY emeralds to pay me.

Then Ziggy said HE hadn't been able to come up with the emeralds either. He moaned something about how hungry he'd been since his family gave up rotten flesh for the holidays. He said he MIGHT have spent all his emeralds in the school vending machine.

GREAT.

And Willow? Turns out, she never even TALKED to her friend with all the little sisters. "I thought you had enough business without me!" she said. Then she mumbled something about having to get home because she'd left a potion brewing and was afraid it would bubble over.

That means I have exactly ZERO emeralds coming my way for this Santa gig. And I've decided I have zero FRIENDS too.

So you know what I'm doing? I'm calling off Christmas. I can do that, you know. A creeper doesn't work for free—not when he has presents to buy for his OWN family.

My 30-day plan just turned into a 7-day plan. I'm going to FORGET Christmas and focus on Creeper's Eve.

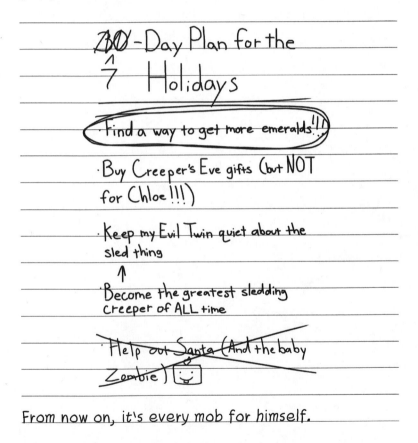

~~30~~ 7 -Day Plan for the Holidays

- (Find a way to get more emeralds!!!)
- Buy Creeper's Eve gifts (but NOT for Chloe!!!)
- Keep my Evil Twin quiet about the sled thing
- Become the greatest sledding creeper of ALL time
- ~~Help out Santa (And the baby Zombie)~~ 😊

From now on, it's every mob for himself.

Ho, ho, ho . . .

DAY 24: SUNDAY (NIGHT)— STILL . . .

After my "friends" left, I marched right back to my room. And managed to trip over one of Cammy's dumb creeper dolls. And broke its leg off. Which felt kind of good for a second, but I knew I had to fix it or Cammy would blow her top.

So while I was sticking that leg back where it belonged, I decided something. I decided that Cammy has the right idea, playing with baby dolls. They do WHATEVER you want them to do. They don't talk back. And they're always smiling.

Not like friends. Or pet SQUIDs, for that matter.

Sticky's been staring at me all night, which is really creeping me out. And he's definitely NOT smiling. "WHAT?" I kept asking him. Part of me wishes he could talk. The other part wishes he'd just shut up already.

Gurgle

I finally stopped looking at him. I have this great ignoring trick where I ALMOST look at him, but I'm really looking just to the right of him. Or to the left of him. Or at the table under his aquarium. Or at the wall above his aquarium.

I've been working on that trick during lunchtime, when I sit next to Ziggy and want to NOT see the food falling out of his mouth. And I have to say, it comes in handy a lot of other times too.

Except tonight, when I looked above Sticky's aquarium, my eyes ran smack into a drawing of a baby zombie and Santa. And then I remembered something.

ZOE.

She thinks Santa IS coming this year! She's probably waiting in her crib with her eyes wide open. Because of Ziggy's big mouth. GREAT.

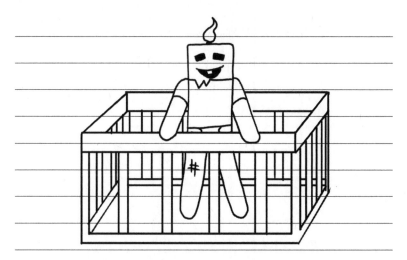

Well, I am NOT going to feel guilty for something Ziggy did. The sun is going to come up any minute now, and I'm going to sleep like a baby—a baby CREEPER, not a baby zombie.

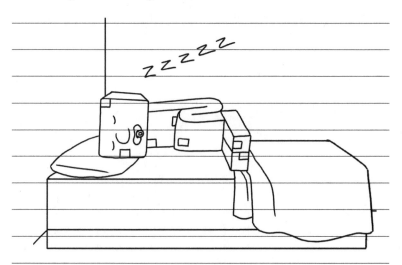

Because everyone knows baby zombies don't sleep.

Especially ones who are waiting for Santa.

DAY 25: MONDAY (YEAH, CHRISTMAS)

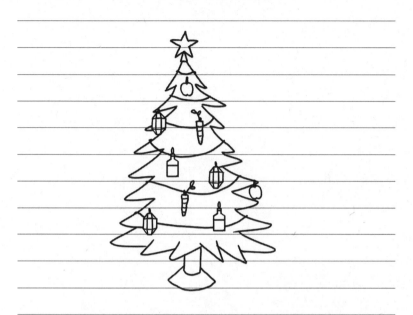

I wish I'd never HEARD of this dumb thing called Christmas. Because if I hadn't, I would have gone to bed at dawn instead of getting up and heading out into the cold.

I wouldn't have walked to school wearing a girl's robe and high-heeled boots. And Eddy Enderman never would have SEEN me wearing a girl's robe and high-heeled boots. And he never would have

seen the DOLL that fell out of my pocket, where I'd
stuffed it after fixing that bum leg.

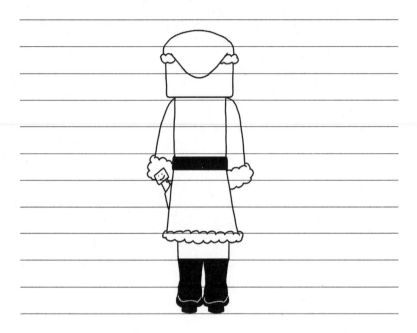

I really appreciate that Eddy didn't mention any of
that. He just pretended he didn't see it.

And it was nice of him to give me extra lessons with
Pearl, because that wolf-dog still wasn't loving me.
Maybe it was because Eddy made her wear skeleton-
bone antlers so she'd look like a real reindeer, and
she blamed ME for that.

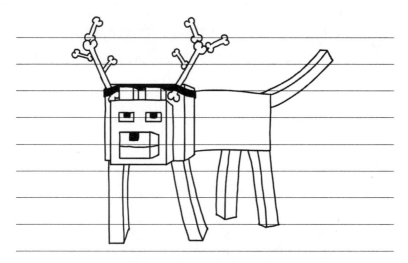

Just like I blamed Ziggy for this whole Santa thing. If he hadn't gone and blabbed to Zoe about Santa coming, I wouldn't even BE in this mess.

Anyway, as soon as it started to rain, Eddy was all like, "I'm out of here, dude."

And then it was just me and the moody wolf-dog wearing antlers. At first, she sat on her butt and refused to go anywhere. But finally, after giving her like THREE bones, I got her to trot toward Ziggy's house, pulling me along in that rusty old minecart.

We were halfway there before I thought of something. Pearl LOOKED like a reindeer, but she couldn't fly like one. How in the Overworld was I supposed to get up on Ziggy's roof so I could slide down his chimney?

Elytra???

I was madder than ever at Ziggy by the time I got to his house, but then I saw something bright and shiny in his front yard. It was a very big, very green slime butt. And I'd know that slime butt anywhere.

Sam the Slime was crawling on the ground under a window. He was wearing that ginormous Santa suit and a long white beard. Was he trying to steal my gig?

I was mad at first, but when Sam saw me, he started blubbering and said he was sorry and was just trying to help. I was afraid he was going to wake up the whole neighborhood, so I accepted his apology.

When he offered me his Santa beard, I put it on. And when he handed me a bottle of fire resistance potion, I took that too. (Thank Golem Willow had sent it with him. I'd totally forgotten about that!)

Then I *thought* of a way Sam could REALLY help.
Bones used to call *him* "Sampoline" because he's
bouncy, like a trampoline. And I needed a trampoline
right about then. So I asked Sam to lie on his
bouncy belly, and I climbed onto his back.

After a few bounces, I actually made it up onto the
chimney.

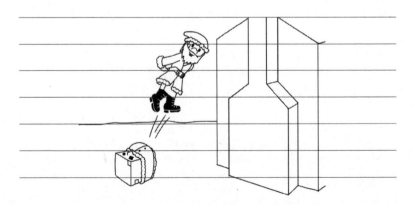

And you can imagine my surprise when I saw a whole lot of NO SMOKE coming out of that chimney. Had Ziggy forgotten to light a lava fire? I KNEW I couldn't count on that worthless zombie!

I was probably going to run into one of Leggy's sticky spider webs in that chimney. And I really didn't have TIME for that right now.

When I peeked down the chimney, I didn't see Leggy, which was a relief. So I finally took a deep breath and climbed in. Actually, I kind of JUMPED in, because I needed some speed to break through any cobwebs. Which meant I slid down that chimney so fast, I ended up skidding out into the middle of the living room floor.

The first thing I heard was a CLUCK. And Zoe's pet chicken strutted into the room. Well, I didn't see THAT coming. How do you keep a watch-chicken quiet?

I tried petting her, which only made her cluck louder.

CLUCK
CLUCK
CLUCK

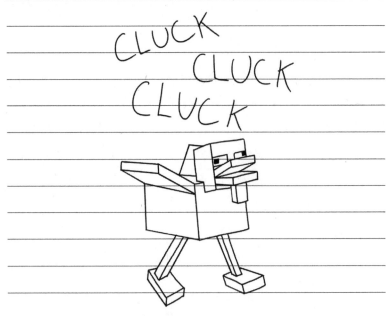

Finally, in a moment of panic, I picked up a piece of rotten flesh from the plate on the table and tossed it to the chicken. And she gobbled it right up. GROSS.

Then I saw the note by the plate of flesh. It said, "For Santa." GREAT. Why can't zombies leave cookies and hot cocoa like everyone else? At least there was a carrot too, which looked pretty delicious next to that rotten flesh.

I ate the carrot in about two bites. Then I tossed the chicken a few more scraps of meat so it would look like Santa had eaten some of that too. And that's when I heard a sound coming from the next room. SINGING.

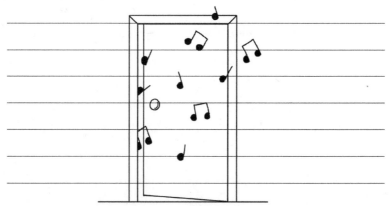

Yup, Zoe the Baby Zombie was wide awake in her bed. And she was singing a song about jingling bells. And riding through the snow in a sleigh. She was singing a CHRISTMAS song.

Well, I knew right then that I had to step it up. I had to get out of that living room before her song ended and she came out to see what all the clucking was about. So I grabbed the apples out of my sweater sack and stuffed them in the socks hanging by the fireplace.

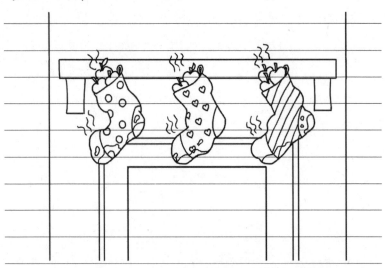

I don't even want to TELL you how old and gross those socks were. They were green. They were stinky.

They were crusty. I had to close my eyes AND my nose to get anywhere near them. Not even an enchanted apple could have made those socks smell better.

But I did my job.

And then I saw the tree. The dead tree. The one that Santa is supposed to put BIG gifts under. How could I have forgotten that???

Something poked my side, and I pulled Cammy's creeper doll out of my pocket. Before I could even think about it, I put that green doll under the tree. Because Zoe needed SOMETHING. I'd just have to figure out how to deal with Cammy's unhappy explosions later.

Then I headed back into the fireplace. But going UP is always harder than going down. I probably would have learned that if I'd taken a Santa class at school or something. But since I was kind of learning on the fly here, I just had to start climbing.

Inch by inch, I worked my way up that chimney. And then, all of a sudden, I couldn't move my feet. Not even an inch.

I was STUCK.

In a spider web.

With no one to cut me out.

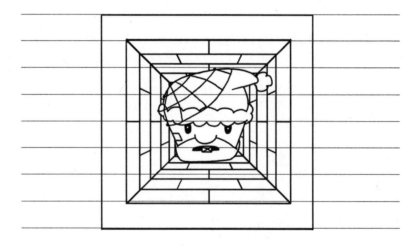

You know those nightmares where you have to MAKE yourself open your eyes to wake up out of it? Well, I kept shutting my eyes and opening them. And nothing happened.

Because it wasn't a nightmare.

It was REAL.

I was actually STUCK in the middle of a zombie fireplace on Christmas. That's not something I could have seen coming if you'd asked me 25 days ago.

So I did what any creeper would do.

I freaked out.

I hissed. I shook. I bubbled. And I blew.

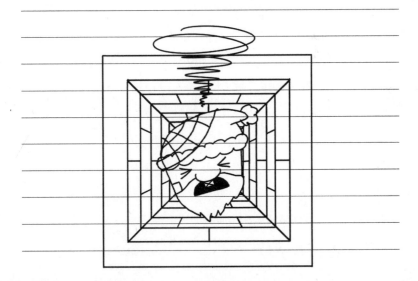

A few bricks tumbled out of the fireplace with me, and a cloud of gunpowder filled the room. But I was FREE.

Until I realized there were four zombies staring at me. Two of them were moaning and rubbing their eyes, looking really confused. One of them was dancing around. He was covering his mouth, trying not to say, "Hey, Gerald! I know it's you!" Yup, that was Ziggy.

And the littlest zombie? She looked right at me through all that gunpowder.

Well, I'd already pretty much blown my gig as Santa, so I didn't want to overstay my welcome. I got out of there ASAP. Through the front door. And I hopped into that minecart faster than you can say, "Ho, ho, ho."

I don't know where Sam was. I didn't even look. I just let Pearl take right turns all the way back to the school. And when she stopped by a tree to rub those dumb antlers off her head, I couldn't blame her. I pulled off my purse hat too. And that white beard, which was probably full of slime snot.

By the time I got home, I'd taken off that robe and those high-heeled boots too. And I crawled into bed with the covers over my head.

Now, while I write all this, a squid is staring at me.
And a wolf-dog too.

I'll have to get her back to Eddy later. Right now,
all this Santa wants to do is sleep—and forget about
the total Christ-MESS he just made.

Wake me up when it's all over, would ya?

DAY 27: WEDNESDAY

Well, let's face it. I'm three days away from Creeper's Eve. And I might as well just call it quits on my 30-day plan.

Why? Because here's what I've accomplished:

~~30~~ 7-Day Plan for the Holidays

- ~~Find a way to get more emeralds!!!~~ *(NOPE!)*
- Buy Creeper's Eve gifts (but NOT for Chloe!!!) *(NOPE)*
- ~~Keep my Evil Twin quiet about the~~ sled thing (WELL YEAH BUT JUST BARELY)
- Become the greatest sledding creeper of ALL time (UM *NO*)
- ~~Help out Santa (And the baby Zombie)~~ 😊 (DOUBLE *NO*. I DON'T EVEN WANT TO TALK ABOUT IT)

Ziggy keeps trying to tell me that I did real good on that last one. He says Zoe was so happy, she hasn't shut up about Santa all week.

I didn't really believe him, so he brought me a new picture she'd made. It shows her next to Santa, just like the other picture she drew. And Santa is standing next to a Christmas tree—Zoe glued a chicken feather to the paper for that and decorated it with sparkles. The feather was already kind of coming unglued, but I still thought that was pretty creative of her.

But here's the biggest thing. In this new picture, Santa is tall and skinny. And very GREEN.

So, I don't know. Maybe I did ONE thing right. But it's not going to help me score points for my family on Creeper's Eve.

I've pretty much given up on earning emeralds to buy gifts, so I'm going to have to make them myself. (I think Zoe's picture gave me that idea.)

I'm sure Chloe will be so disgusted by a handmade gift from me, she'll open her mouth and blab to my parents about everything I did wrong. But if she does, that's okay.

Being Chloe's slave is kind of like being stuck in a spider web. Sometimes you just have to bust out, let the gunpowder fall, and then move on.

DAY 31: SUNDAY (CREEPER'S EVE)

Well, *huh.* That didn't go NEARLY as badly as I thought it would.

I *spent all day* yesterday working on making gifts for my family. I stayed in my room, and no one bugged me—maybe because they were working on Creeper's Eve stuff too.

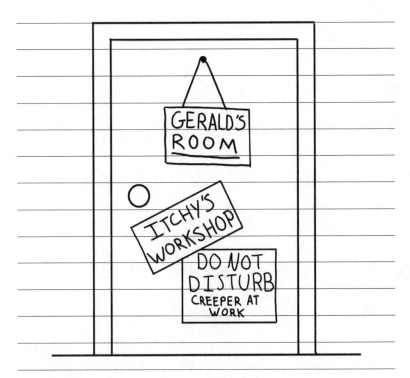

When I told Mom I had to use the kitchen for a secret project, that made her really happy. She stayed out of my way—I mean, except for when I set off the smoke alarm. Then she came running back in, but she promised not to look at what came out of the oven as long as I took it out RIGHT AWAY.

When the sun came up, Dad hollered, "Bedtime! Creepers need their sleepers!" He just LOVES sneaking around and hiding gifts.

I tried to stay awake. I sat in bed, listening to my family's footsteps as they tiptoed around hiding gifts. But I guess making presents is exhausting stuff, because I ended up falling asleep. When I woke up, it was still daytime, thank goodness. So I got up and quickly hid my presents too.

I didn't put a lot of thought into hiding places. I just picked out my five oldest socks—the ones that didn't have holes in them. And I hung them by the fireplace. Then I stuck the presents inside.

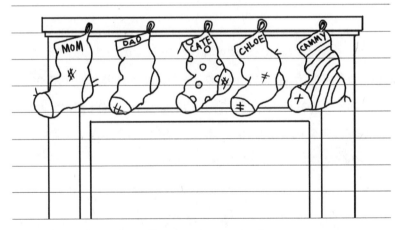

Tonight, when we all got up, Mom let us eat our fried eggs and roasted potatoes in the living room. And then we opened presents.

Well, my family was sure surprised by those socks I gave them (or STOCKINGS, as Ziggy would say).

Mom really liked the potion of fire resistance I put inside hers.

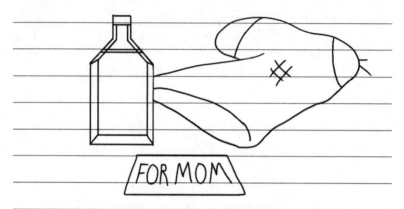

It was the bottle Willow gave me, but I figured it would help Mom deal with all of Cammy's explosions. I wrote a note telling her she was a good mom and deserved a little help, and I think she got kind of weepy-eyed when she read that.

I wrote a rap song and put that inside Dad's stocking. I promised to perform it for him after dinner, and he thought that was pretty cool.

I gave Cate the white Santa beard from Sam, because he said I could keep it. (I didn't tell her about the slime snot that had gotten all over it during his emotional breakdown on Christmas.) At first, she didn't know why I was giving her a beard. Then I showed her how she could turn it upside down like a wig. So now she has a white wig like the one she cut up to make into my Santa suit!

I gave Cammy the little feather Christmas tree that Zoe tried to glue to her picture. It was so pretty, with all those sprinkles. And Cammy really liked it. I could tell, because she ALMOST exploded.

Well, I saved Chloe for last, because she was the HARDEST one. I hadn't really wanted to give her anything, but then I'd gotten an idea. A pretty creative idea.

Her present was too big to put in a stocking, so I put some clues in her stocking instead. The clues led her through the house and out to the garage. And THERE was my green sled with a big red bow on it. Sam helped me clean it up so it looked brand new.

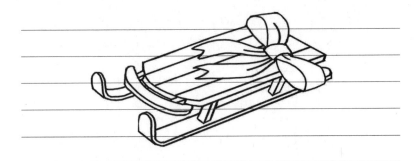

I sure was gonna miss that sled. But I figured if I gave it to Chloe, she couldn't tell Mom and Dad that I'd blown my emeralds on it. Genius, right?

Except my twin had a surprise for me too. She said I should open my present from her and Dad right away, which was hiding under my bed.

I don't know HOW they got it under there while I was sleeping. But it doesn't really matter. Because you want to know what the present was?

A SLED. Just as shiny and green as the one I'd given Chloe.

TWINNING

I didn't know if my twin was trying to trick me or what. Did she think I'd start to sweat when I saw that sled? Did she think I'd blow sky high?

I stared at her, trying to figure it out. But she just smiled sweetly and said, "Merry Creeper's Eve." Maybe my gift to her had softened her up. Maybe she was happy now that SHE had a sled too. Anyway, I'm not going to question her niceness—at least not until the new year.

After we opened all the presents, I served up my last surprise: an apple-carrot cake. I didn't used to be big on carrots, but now they kind of remind me of Zoe and her plate of treats for Santa. And while we snacked on the cake, I told my family all about Christmas.

Mom said it didn't sound all that different from Creeper's Eve—that most holidays were about giving things up (like rotten flesh and stinky old socks) and doing nice things for family and friends.

She might be right about that.

But I reminded her that holidays are ALSO about miracles. Because right in the middle of performing my rap for Dad, I looked up and saw something falling outside the window.

Something white. Something wet. Something wonderful.

It was SNOWING again.

Just in time.

Rappin' through the snow
In a one-wolf open sleigh
Over the plains we go
Rappin' all the way.

HO, HO, HO!